Hamsters invented EVERYTHING

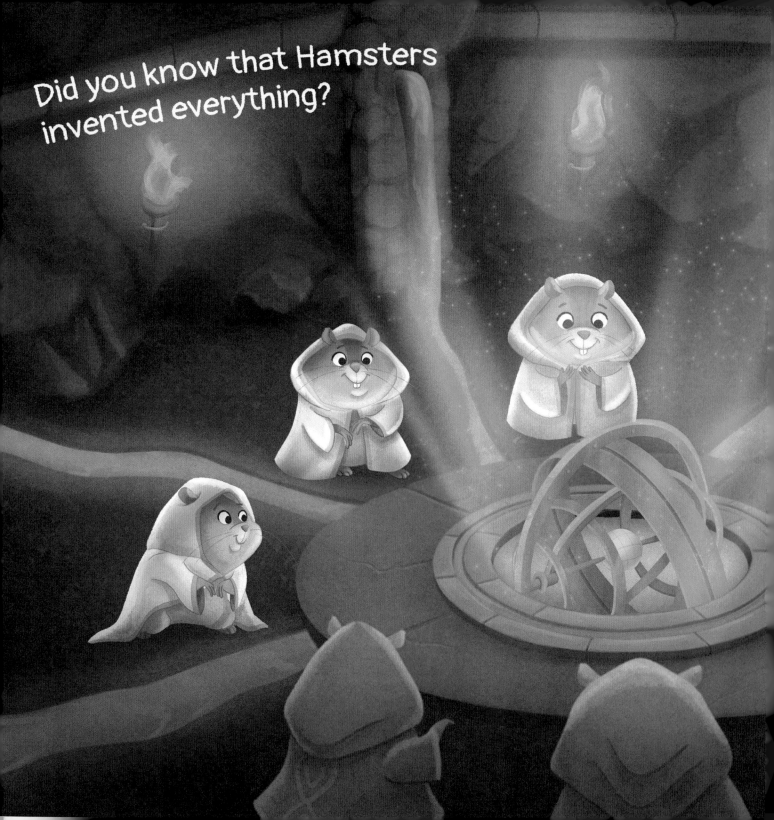

Did you know that Hamsters invented everything?

It's a secret that most humans don't know about, but they've had an underground society since the dawn of time and have invented literally EVERYTHING.

The laws of gravity?

It was a Hamster that gave the idea to Isaac Newton!

Sneakers?

Actually, that was a human, but Hamsters invented the laces, which were the most important part of sneakers being created. So they sort of invented that one too.

Foxes, the sworn enemies of Hamsters, have always tried to stop Hamsters from sharing their inventions with humans.

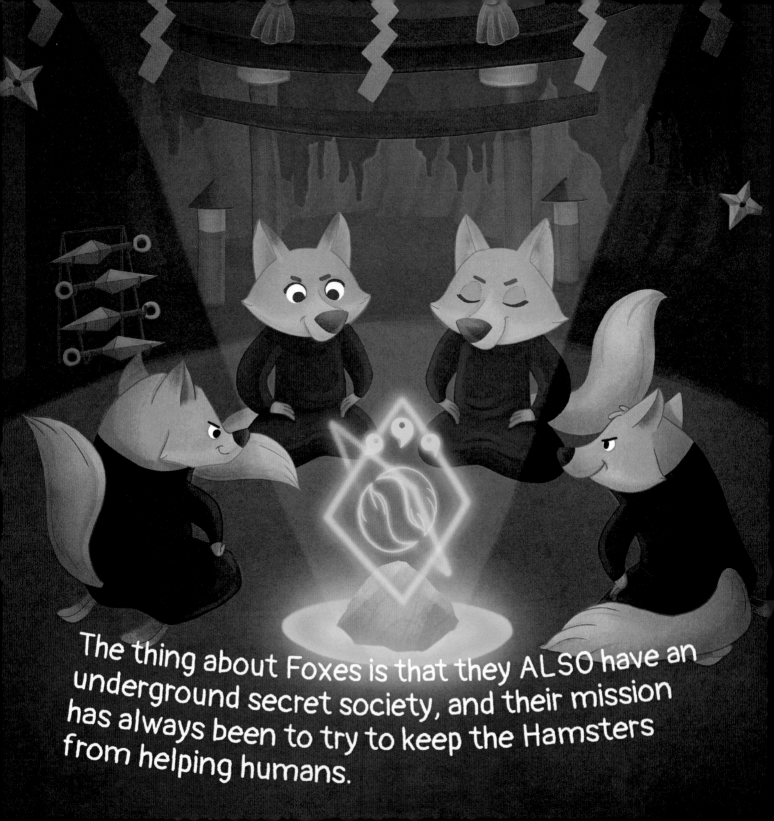

The thing about Foxes is that they ALSO have an underground secret society, and their mission has always been to try to keep the Hamsters from helping humans.

When the Hamsters tried to share the wheel?

Yep, look closer...a Fox.

The printing press?
Telescopes?
Computers?
Spaceships?

But the real problem was that Foxes had just stolen the most important invention in history. One that the Hamsters had not yet shared with humans. A spaceship engine that allowed travel between planets!

With this technology, the Foxes planned to take over the universe as we know it!

It was decided that secret Hamster agents, who were already in every 3rd grade classroom, would be the first to speak to humans.

At first, the humans didn't know how to react. It was on every news channel and all over the internet.

The plan was set.
The Hamsters knew
that the drawings for
the spaceship engine were stored deep in
the Foxes' top secret lab...inside a volcano!

The humans would surround the Foxes' lair. Then the Hamsters would be dropped in by helicopter to take the plans before the Foxes could use them.

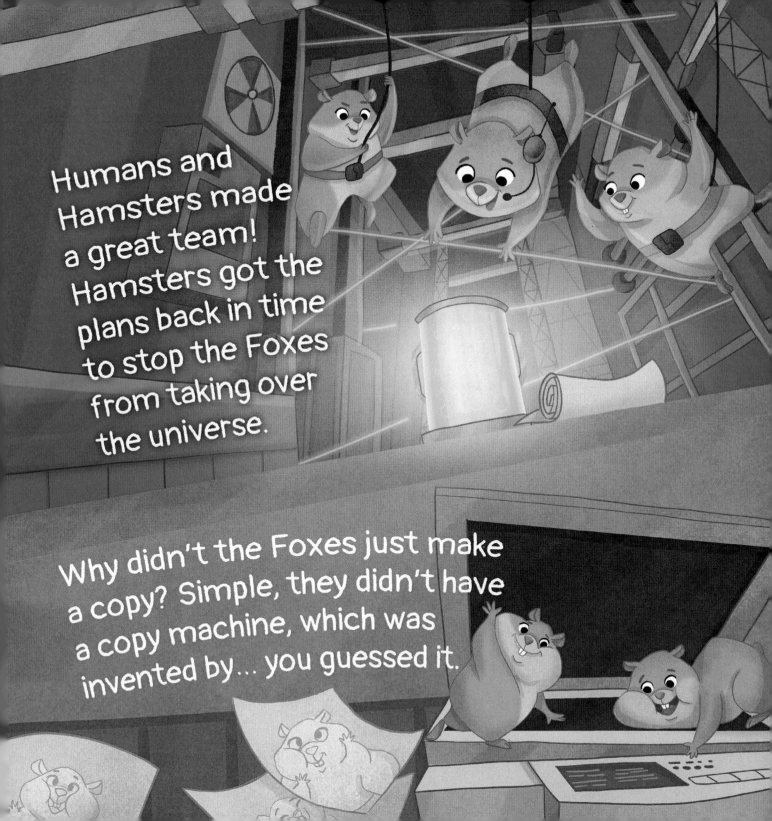

Humans and Hamsters made a great team! Hamsters got the plans back in time to stop the Foxes from taking over the universe.

Why didn't the Foxes just make a copy? Simple, they didn't have a copy machine, which was invented by... you guessed it.

Humans, thankful for all that the Hamsters had done, decided to change their history books to give Hamsters the credit they deserved.

All secret Hamster agents assigned to 3rd grade classes were rewarded extra carrots and cabbage on a daily basis.

Hamster spas, filled with hamster wheels as far as the eye could see, were made to be free for all Hamsters.

It was a golden age for humans and Hamsters. Information was shared between the two species and there was progress in every area of science

All was well in the world and the Foxes retreated back to their holes...for now.

Check out our other great books!

Available on Amazon

Made in the USA
Las Vegas, NV
08 February 2023